EPISODE VI
RETURN OF THE JEDI

BASED ON A STORY BY
GEORGE LUCAS

SCRE[...]
LAWREN[...]

GEOR[...] LUCAS

HAMBURG • LONDON • LOS ANGELES • TOKYO

Editor - Rob Tokar
Contributing Editor - Mad Science Media
Graphic Designers and Letterers - Tomás Montalvo-Lagos and John Lo
Cover Designer - Raymond Makowski
Graphic Artist - Louis Csontos

Digital Imaging Manager - Chris Buford
Pre-Press Manager - Antonio DePietro
Production Managers - Jennifer Miller and Mutsumi Miyazaki
Senior Designer - Anna Kernbaum
Art Director - Matt Alford
Senior Editor - Elizabeth Hurchalla
Managing Editor - Jill Freshney
VP of Production - Ron Klamert
Editor-in-Chief - Mike Kiley
President & C.O.O. - John Parker
Publisher & C.E.O. - Stuart Levy

E-mail: info@tokyopop.com
Come visit us online at www.TOKYOPOP.com

A ⓒ TOKYOPOP Cine-Manga® Book
TOKYOPOP Inc.
5900 Wilshire Blvd., Suite 2000
Los Angeles, CA 90036

Star Wars: Return of the Jedi

Special thanks to Paul Southern, Amy Gary,
Sue Rostoni and Valentina Dose.

ISBN: 1-59532-897-1

First TOKYOPOP® printing: May 2005

10 9 8 7 6 5 4 3 2 1

Printed in China

LUKE SKYWALKER:
JEDI KNIGHT-
IN-TRAINING.

DARTH VADER:
LORD OF THE SITH

HAN SOLO:
SMUGGLER

CHEWBACCA:
WOOKIEE AND
HAN SOLO'S PARTNER

LEIA ORGANA:
PRINCESS AND
REBEL LEADER

SEE-THREEPIO (C-3PO):
PROTOCOL DROID

ARTOO-DETOO (R2-D2):
ASTROMECH DROID AND
SEE-THREEPIO'S SIDEKICK

YODA:
JEDI MASTER

A long time ago in a galaxy far, far away....

Luke Skywalker has returned to his home planet of Tatooine in an attempt to rescue his friend Han Solo from the clutches of the vile gangster Jabba the Hutt.

Little does Luke know that the GALACTIC EMPIRE has secretly begun construction on a new armored space station even more powerful than the first dreaded Death Star.

When completed, this ultimate weapon will spell certain doom for the small band of Rebels struggling to restore freedom to the galaxy....

Commander, I'm here to put you back on schedule.

But the Emperor asks the impossible. I need more men.

Then perhaps you can tell him when he arrives.

The Emperor's coming here? We shall double our efforts!

I hope so, Commander, for your sake.

THIS CAN'T BE! ARTOO, YOU'RE PLAYING THE WRONG MESSAGE.

<There will be no bargain.>

<I will not give up my favorite decoration. I like Captain Solo where he is.>

ARTOO, LOOK! CAPTAIN SOLO-- AND HE'S STILL FROZEN IN CARBONITE.

THE DROIDS ARE SPLIT UP AND C-3PO IS ASSIGNED TO BE JABBA'S TRANSLATOR...

...BUT C-3PO'S FIRST ASSIGNMENT TURNS INTO AN UNEXPECTED REUNION...

We have powerful friends. You're gonna regret this.

<I'm sure.>

DEEP IN THE BOWELS OF JABBA'S PALACE, HAN IS THROWN INTO CHEWBACCA'S CELL.

Rahrr!

Chewie? Is that you?

Ruhrr whar rurah rff!

Luke? He can't even take care of himself, much less rescue anybody.

A--a Jedi Knight? I'm out of it for a little while, and everybody gets delusions of grandeur.

Rarr ruh rffr ruhh!

LATER. IN JABBA'S MAIN AUDIENCE CHAMBER...

You will bring Captain Solo and the Wookiee to me.

<Your mind powers will not work on me, boy.>

Nevertheless, I'm taking Captain Solo and his friends.

You can either profit by this...or be destroyed. It's your choice. But I warn you not to underestimate my powers.

<There will be no bargain, young Jedi. I shall enjoy watching you die!>

AT JABBA'S COMMAND. THE FLOOR SUDDENLY DROPS AWAY BENEATH LUKE AND A HAPLESS GUARD WHO FIND THEMSELVES TUMBLING INTO A PIT BELOW.

GRAHHH!

AFTER QUICKLY DEVOURING THE GUARD, THE CREATURE WITHIN SEEKS ITS NEXT VICTIM...

GRAHHH!

RORAAH--

THINKING FAST, LUKE BRINGS A HEAVY DOOR CRASHING DOWN ON THE CREATURE'S SKULL.

--AHRRR!!

WATCHING FROM THE FLOOR ABOVE...

<Bring me Solo and the Wookiee. They will all suffer for this outrage!>

SOON, BACK IN JABBA'S THRONE ROOM...

OH DEAR. JABBA HAS DECREED THAT YOU ARE TO BE TAKEN TO THE DUNE SEA AND CAST INTO THE NESTING PLACE OF THE SARLACC.

IN HIS BELLY, YOU WILL FIND A NEW DEFINITION OF SUFFERING, AS YOU ARE SLOWLY DIGESTED OVER A THOUSAND YEARS.

Let's pass on that, huh?

You should have bargained, Jabba. That's the last mistake you'll ever make.

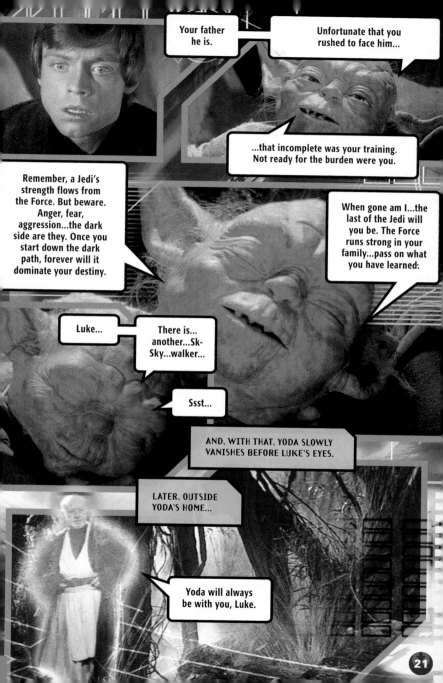

The Death Star is protected by an energy shield, which is generated from the nearby forest moon of Endor.

Once we deactivate the shield, our fighters will fly into the superstructure and attack the main reactor. General Calrissian has volunteered to lead the assault.

GENERAL MADINE OUTLINES THE REST OF THE ATTACK PLAN...

We have stolen a small Imperial shuttle. Disguised as a cargo ship and using a secret Imperial code, a strike team will land on the moon and deactivate the shield generator.

General Solo, is your strike team assembled?

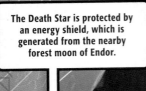

SHORTLY, ABOARD THE STOLEN IMPERIAL SHUTTLE, THE VOLUNTEER COMMAND CREW PREPS FOR LAUNCH.

Ready, everybody?

Let's see what this piece of junk can do.

LUKE AND LEIA JUMP ON A PARKED SPEEDER BIKE...

Get alongside that one!

JUMPING FROM THEIR SPEEDER BIKE, LUKE COMMANDEERS THE TROOPER'S.

HOWEVER, THAT JUST GIVES THE SCOUT TROOPERS BEHIND THE TWO REBELS MORE TARGETS TO SHOOT!

Keep on the one ahead, Leia...

THE SCOUT TROOPER USES HIS SIDEARM TO KNOCK LEIA FROM HER SPEEDER...

...THOUGH THE DISTRACTION DOES FAR WORSE TO HIM!

THE FIREBALL CREATED BY HER OPPONENT'S CRASH...

...IS THE LAST THING LEIA SEES BEFORE LOSING CONSCIOUSNESS.

MEANWHILE, LUKE'S OPPONENT FORCES HIM TO HURL HIMSELF OFF HIS SPEEDER BIKE TO AVOID A CRASH.

THE SCOUT TROOPER CIRCLES BACK TO MAKE THE KILL...

...BUT THE YOUNG JEDI'S LIGHTSABER DEFLECTS HIS BLASTER BOLTS...

...AS EASILY AS IT SLICES OFF THE SPEEDER BIKE'S STEERING VANES!

Whew.

LATER, AT THE EWOKS' TREETOP VILLAGE...

...THE REBELS ARE REUNITED WITH LEIA AS C-3PO TELLS THE TALE OF THE GALACTIC CIVIL WAR.

AND, AFTER A BRIEF CONFERENCE OF THE EWOK LEADERSHIP...

WONDERFUL! WE ARE NOW A PART OF THE TRIBE. TOMORROW THE SCOUTS ARE GOING TO SHOW US THE QUICKEST WAY TO THE SHIELD GENERATOR.

OUTSIDE...

Luke, tell me. What's troubling you?

Vader is here...now, on this moon. He can feel when I'm near.

I have to face him.

MEANWHILE, ON ENDOR, THE REBELS TAKE CONTROL OF THE BUNKER THAT HOUSES THE DEFLECTOR SHIELD GENERATOR...

Han! Hurry! The fleet will be here any moment.

Charges! Come on, come on!

BUT...

Freeze! You Rebel scum.

HIDDEN IN THE FOREST OUTSIDE, C-3PO, R2-D2 AND AN EWOK WITNESS A MASS OF IMPERIAL STORMTROOPERS RETAKING THE BASE!

OH, MY! THEY'LL BE CAPTURED!

Eee jomama! Hata hata!

W-WAIT! WAIT-- COME BACK!

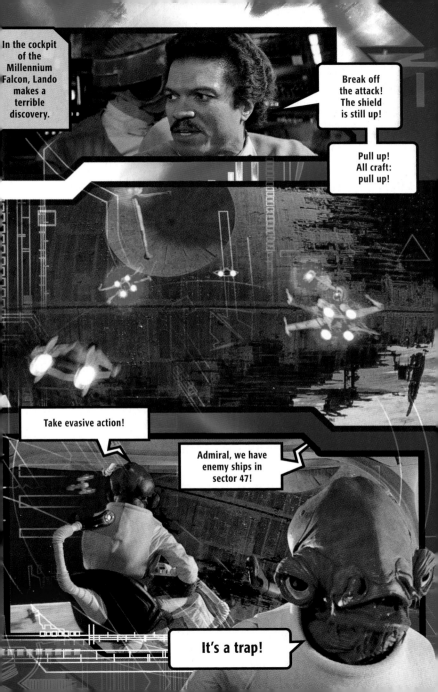

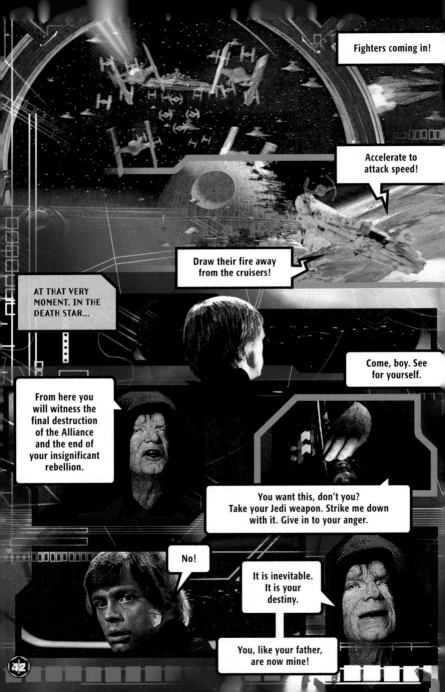

FAR BELOW, ON THE SURFACE OF THE FOREST MOON...

Move it!

HELLO! I SAY, OVER THERE!

WERE YOU LOOKING FOR ME?

Bring those two down here!

Freeze! Don't move!

WE SURRENDER.

SUDDENLY...

AIIEEE YAHHH!

43

GRABBING WEAPONS FROM THEIR CAPTORS...

...HAN AND LEIA FEROCIOUSLY FIGHT THEIR WAY BACK TO THE BUNKER DOORS.

The code's changed!

Artoo, we need you at the bunker right away!

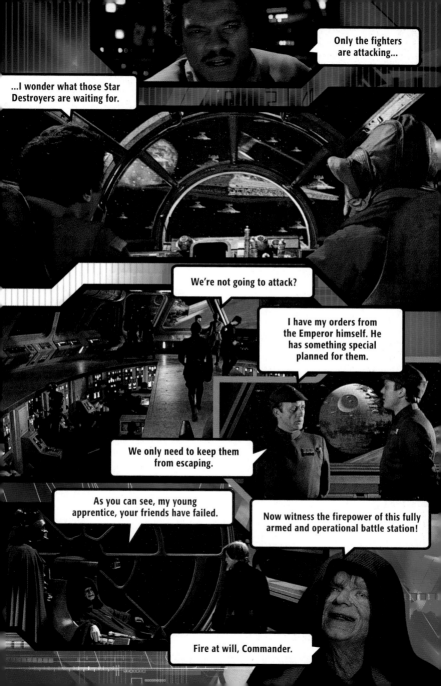

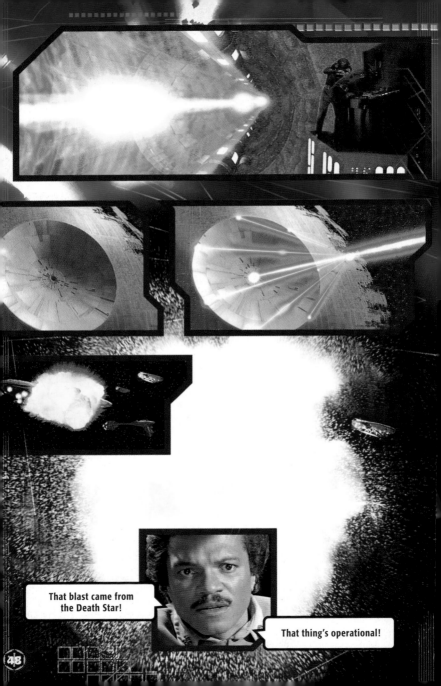

That blast came from the Death Star!

That thing's operational!

Home One, this is Gold Leader.

We saw it. All craft prepare to retreat.

You won't get another chance at this, Admiral.

We have no choice, General Calrissian. Our cruisers can't repel firepower of that magnitude.

Han will have that shield down! We've got to give him more time!

IN THE FOREST SURROUNDING THE SHIELD GENERATOR, IMPERIAL SCOUT WALKERS WREAK HAVOC.

Yug Yug!

Aaaah!

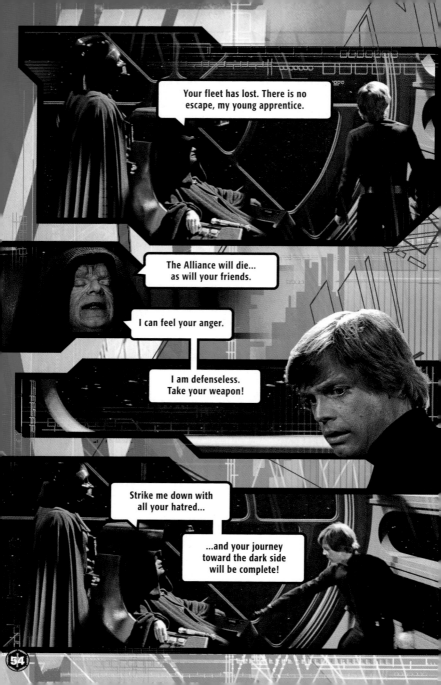

HA HA HA HA!

ON THE FOREST MOON...

RRRAAHW!

CHEWBACCA AND TWO EWOKS COMMANDEER AN ARMORED SCOUT WALKER...

...AND RETALIATE!

56

UAAAAH!!

Let's see.

It's not bad.

Freeze! Don't move!

THOUGH HIS BODY BLOCKS THE STORMTROOPERS' VIEW, HAN EASILY SPIES THE CONTENTS OF LEIA'S HAND.

60

THE YOUNG JEDI MAKES AN IMPOSSIBLE BACKFLIP UP TO THE SAFETY OF A NEARBY CATWALK AND AGAIN DEACTIVATES HIS WEAPON...

Your thoughts betray you, Father.

I feel the good in you...the conflict.

There is no conflict.

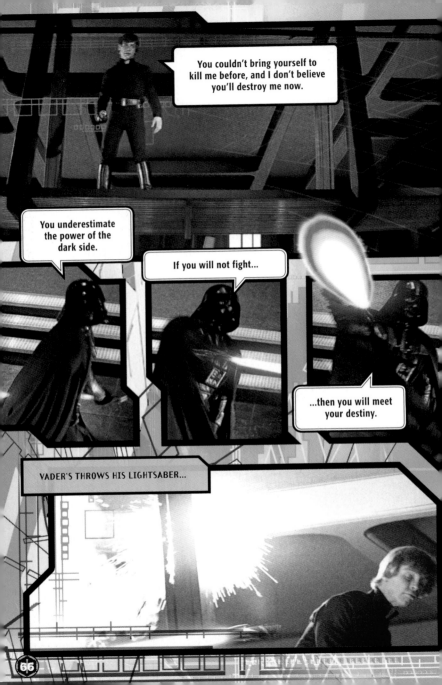

Good! Your hate has made you powerful.

Now, fulfill your destiny and take your father's place at my side!

73

If you will not be turned...

...you will be destroyed.

GAHHH!

AAGH!

Young fool...only now, at the end, do you understand.

Your feeble skills are no match for the power of the dark side!

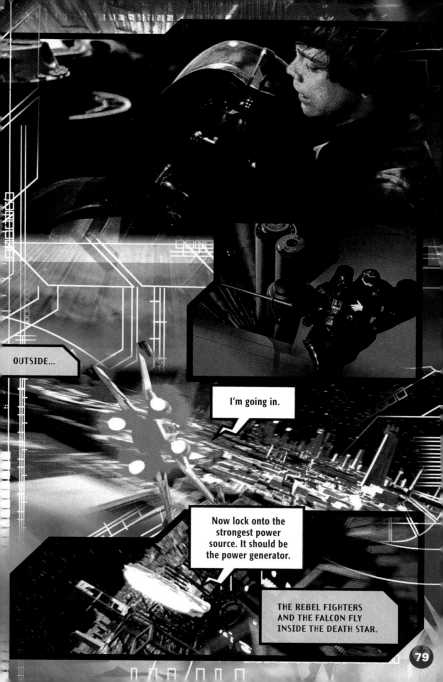

OUTSIDE...

I'm going in.

Now lock onto the strongest power source. It should be the power generator.

THE REBEL FIGHTERS AND THE FALCON FLY INSIDE THE DEATH STAR.

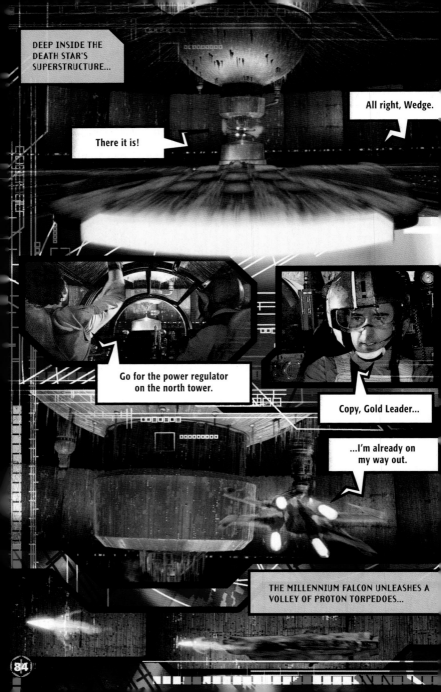

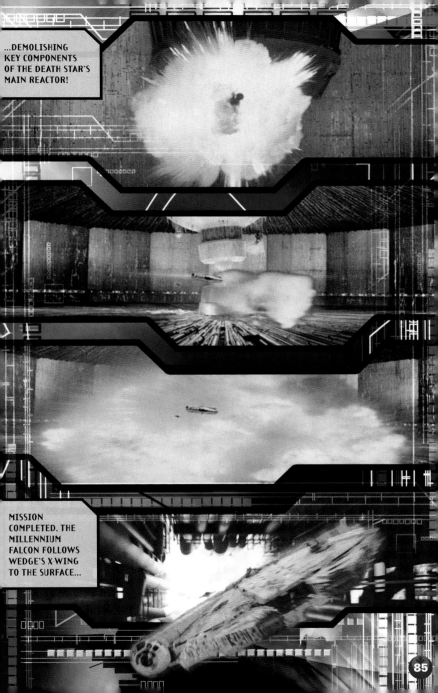

...DEMOLISHING KEY COMPONENTS OF THE DEATH STAR'S MAIN REACTOR!

MISSION COMPLETED, THE MILLENNIUM FALCON FOLLOWS WEDGE'S X-WING TO THE SURFACE...

...WHILE LUKE STEALS AN IMPERIAL SHUTTLE...

...AND THE REBEL FLEET MOVES TO A SAFE DISTANCE AWAY FROM THE DEATH STAR.

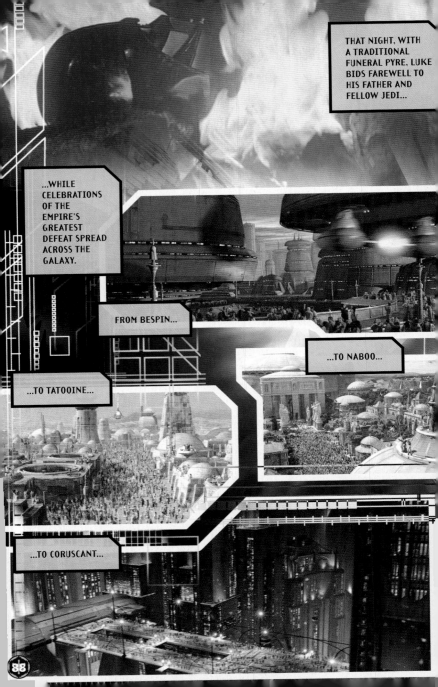

THAT NIGHT, WITH A TRADITIONAL FUNERAL PYRE, LUKE BIDS FAREWELL TO HIS FATHER AND FELLOW JEDI...

...WHILE CELEBRATIONS OF THE EMPIRE'S GREATEST DEFEAT SPREAD ACROSS THE GALAXY.

FROM BESPIN...

...TO NABOO...

...TO TATOOINE...

...TO CORUSCANT...

STAR WARS VEHICLES

The gentle Mon Calamari people brought more than their determination to restore freedom to the galaxy when they joined the Rebel Alliance. They also brought a fleet of powerful ships that pack an enormous punch. Turbolasers, ion cannons, tractor beam projectors and shield generators dot the flowing surface of the ships. Perhaps the most important Mon Cal cruiser during the Galactic Civil War was the Home One, the headquarters frigate that served as Admiral Ackbar's flagship.

MON CALAMARI STAR CRUISER

ESCORT FRIGATE

Unlike the Empire, which had a galaxy of resources to draw upon, the Rebellion was hard-pressed to equip its soldiers and fleets. The Alliance operated what few cruisers they had nonstop, often modifying them to fit mission profiles beyond their original specifications.

A—WING STARFIGHTERS

Faster than even the TIE interceptor, the A-wing is well suited for lightning strikes. It sports a pair of pivoting laser cannons on each wingtip. The starfighters of Green Squadron, which flew in the Battle of Endor, were made up of A-wing starfighters.

REBEL MEDIUM TRANSPORT

Rebel transports are no-frills vessels that are little more than flying cargo carriages equipped with hyperdrives. The open underbelly of the Rebel medium transport has room for scores of cargo containers. The vessels have minimal armament and are relatively slow.

B—WING STARFIGHTER

Perhaps the oddest looking starfighter in the Rebel Alliance fleet, the B-wing fighter is as powerful as it is ungainly. The B-wing's command pod has a unique gyroscopic control system. The pilot can orient it so that it always stays level with a predesignated horizon line. No matter which way the B-wing may maneuver laterally, its pilot remains upright.

The triangular silhouette of an Imperial cruiser has
come a long way since its Republic-inspired design. The
Imperial Star Destroyer's gargantuan size clearly inspires
both awe and terror. This wedge-shaped capital ship is
bristling with weapons emplacements. Turbolasers and
tractor beam projectors dot its surface. Its ventral bay can
launch TIE fighters, boarding craft, land assault units or
hyperspace probes, or be used to hold captured craft.

The Lambda-class shuttle is a multipurpose transport used in the Imperial Starfleet. When in flight, the side wings fold out for greater stabilization. When landing, the wings fold in, shrinking the vessel's silhouette. The well-equipped vessel has two forward-facing double laser cannons, two wing-mounted double cannons, and a rear-facing double laser cannon. It is equipped with a hyperdrive.

IMPERIAL LAMBDA-CLASS SHUTTLE

A later addition to the TIE (Twin Ion Engine) starfighter arsenal, the TIE interceptor sports a jagged pair of dagger-like wings, giving it an ultrasleek profile that hints at the blinding speed the fighter possesses. Unlike the TIE fighter, the interceptor has four powerful laser cannons mounted on the tips of the dagger wings.

TIE INTERCEPTOR

STAR WARS

Coming to the Cine-Manga® Galaxy!

STAR WARS: A New Hope

STAR WARS: The Empire Strikes Back

THE EMPIRE STRIKES BACK

CINE-MANGA®

NOW IN STORES!

STAR WARS
RETURN OF THE JEDI

STAR WARS: Return of the Jedi

CINE-MANGA

STAR WARS
CLONE WARS

The Clone Wars ar
spreading like a fir
across the galaxy

now in
stores